# UNBORTION

Rowland Bercy Jr.

ISBN- 978-1-7267-4969-5

## ACKNOWLEDGMENTS

Thank you Rowland Bercy Sr.
for being such an amazing role model.

Thank you Raquel Bercy
for challenging me and keeping me laughing.

Thank you Shawn Scott
For being so supportive and putting up with me.

Thank you Chiara Noemi Monaco
for the amazing cover art.

## TRIGGER WARNING / AUTHOR'S NOTE

PLEASE BE AWARE THAT CHAPTER ONE OF UNBORTION CONTAINS A GRAPHIC AND POTENTIALLY DISTRESSING DESCRIPTION OF A PROFESIONALLY-PERFORMED ABORTION.

SENSITIVE READERS SHOULD SKIP THE FIRST FEW PARAGRAPHS AND BEGIN READING WITH THE LAST PARAGRAPH OF CHAPTER ONE TO AVOID ENCOUNTERING ANY POTENTIALLY UPSETTING MATERIAL.

1

It was alive and just getting accustomed to the strange feeling of floating weightlessly supported by amniotic fluid. Even though its eyelids were still shut, it could see light filtering in from outside the womb. As it took breaths, swallowing gulps of amniotic fluid, it became familiar with its own scent. It could hear and was getting used to the strange but muffled sounds surrounding it: the gurgle of the stomach; the whooshing of air in and out of lungs; the soothing sound of the voice of its host. It was also becoming aware of its tiny appendages. It had a sense of touch and would respond to being stimulated within the uterus, and it could feel; but this feeling was different. It was cold, hard, and unrelenting; then, all of a sudden, there was a new feeling: pain! Something had clamped down on its tiny leg and without warning twisted and ripped its leg from its tiny, soft, still developing body. If it could cry, it would. If it could scream out at the top of its underdeveloped lungs, it would, but there was no fighting this onslaught.

Again, the claw reached up and grabbed more of its body, this time gripping right below where its belly button would be. Another pull and its fragile abdomen was torn apart and dragged out along with its other leg. This continued until only the head remained. Lastly, its little skull was crushed and pulled out. Though it should be dead by now, it wasn't; it was fully awake and aware of what was happening to it. It was being destroyed. It was being discarded like unwanted trash.

When the dilation and evacuation was complete, the shady, unethical abortionist then used a technique known as vacuum aspiration, which was completely unnecessary, to collect any remaining pieces. A hollow plastic tube with a knife-like edge was inserted back into the uterus, and then suction was used to vacuum out any remaining body pieces into a collection jar. Next, the placenta was cut from the uterine wall, which was also sucked into the collection bottle. The larger pieces were added to the bottle, making a goulash of fetus body parts, placenta remnants, blood, guts, amniotic sac and fluid. Then the procedure was complete. "Nurse, please see to the remains." The nurse covered the collection jar and exited the room. "Okay, Ms. Miller; we're all done. How are you feeling?" asked the doctor. "Numb," said Ashley. "That's to be expected," said the doctor. "You might experience some abdominal cramping, similar to menstrual cramps, which could last from several hours to a few days, along with some possible vaginal bleeding or spotting, nausea, and/or vomiting." "If any of these signs persist for more than a few days, be sure to give me a call. Also, please be sure to take the antibiotics we gave you to prevent any possible infection." Ashley thanked the abortionist, who then left the room; she proceeded to get dressed and walked out of the building in a daze to the car where her best friend was waiting to drive her home.

"Okay, Megan; she's gone," said the doctor "What did you do with it?" The nurse came in from the back room, smiling. "The same thing I did with all the others. Put it in the dumpster out back with the leftover spaghetti I had for lunch." They both giggled at that. "It was genius telling her that we would have to do suction and aspiration in addition to D&E to make sure all the fetal matter was removed, another easy $600 in our pocket." Megan smiled. "Kids these days don't have a clue. How do you want to celebrate?" asked the doctor with a sly grin on his face. Megan walked up to the doctor. She slid her hands down the front of his pants and grabbed his cock: "Why don't we go into your office and I can show you better than tell you how I want to celebrate."

Not thirty minutes ago, it was warm and safe, tucked away in its host body. Growing accustomed to its host and feeling a stronger and deeper connection to its host day by day, but somehow and for some reason things changed and they changed quickly. It was no longer floating safely, protected by amniotic fluid; instead it was violently ripped from its host and dumped someplace dark, cold, and smelly. And though it should be nothing but a pile of shredded body parts left to be devoured by maggots in the dumpster, it was somehow still alive. Its tiny undeveloped eyes could clearly see. Its fleshy, mangled body parts were strong and operable. It was a blob of connective tissue, discarded placenta, amniotic sac, blood, guts, viscous fluids, and baby body parts. All of the remains were disordered and mashed together into a pile of goop. Somehow the parts were still connected and able to work together, contracting and expanding, allowing the fetus to push and/or pull itself in whatever direction it needed to go, and permitting it to extend its appendages, still attached by connective tissue, placenta, and amniotic sac in multiple directions, well beyond its normal limits. In addition to all of its other senses and the miracle of somehow still being alive, though terribly mangled and disfigured, the fetus could still feel a connection to the host who had forsaken it. Somehow it sensed she was out there somewhere, and it knew instinctively that it could not deny this irrefutable association and would seek her out. "Maybe if I could find her, she would understand what a terrible decision she has made and would welcome me back," thought the fetus to itself, but "when I do find her, if she still tries to deny me, I will make her pay.

## 2

His hair was matted and lice-ridden, and he had long ago become accustomed to the putrid stench of his unwashed body and rags. Leonard had been homeless for the past fifteen years and was by now quite acclimated to his meager lifestyle. No stranger to the stares of passersby, who more often than not crossed the street to avoid him, he had long ago given up on begging. His daily routine for food was to scrounge for scraps in dumpsters, in dark and smelly alley ways of the city. It was late, and most of the street lights had been broken out by the hoodlums who often hung out in the alley during the day, skipping school. Leonard knew this particular alley was prime hunting ground for A-1 scraps as there were plenty of restaurants in the area. The first two dumpsters he scavenged through did not contain much of use. He did find a pair of slightly used, skid-marked underwear, which were ten times cleaner than the one he was presently wearing.

He was just about to give up rummaging through the dumpster, ready to accept the fact that it was going to be yet another night when he would slumber famished when he spied a plastic bag from an Italian restaurant with what looked to be a take-out container. Leonard picked up the bag. It was heavy; that was a good sign. Upon opening the bag, as far as he could make out in the darkness, all the contents of the to-go container had spilled out, and the aroma of spaghetti, mixed with some other pungent stench, which he assumed to be parmesan cheese, filled his nostrils. "Woo-hoo, jackpot!" Leonard thought to himself. "I'll be eating good tonight." Leonard sat down on a crate, which was next to the dumpster and reached for his grungy backpack. He was sure he had a fork somewhere in there. After finding his fork, Leonard emptied the spaghetti from the bag back into the take-out container thinking to himself: "This has got to be the thickest tomato sauce ever." While stirring the spaghetti, he noticed what he thought were chunks of sausage or some other type of meat. Leonard scooped a big fork full of gooey tomato sauce, a small piece of bloody pink sausage and spaghetti then brought the take-out container closer to his mouth; after all, he wouldn't want to get tomato sauce all over his clothes. Just as he opened his mouth and was about to shove a forkful of tasty spaghetti into his filthy cavity-filled maw, Leonard noticed movement on his fork. For a brief moment he thought that maybe a roach or some other insect had gotten into the bag from the dumpster. Just then two tiny hands shot out, one from the fork and the other from the container he held in his hand. Leonard screamed, falling backward off the crate, and tried to throw the container as far away from him as possible. Spaghetti flew everywhere.

The fetus, not knowing what was happening but seeing what it thought was the opportunity to find another host, instinctively reached its sawed and broken off arms out from the spaghetti it had gotten thrown out with. Faster than Leonard could toss it away, one hand still attached by placenta gripped the top of Leonard's mouth and the other attached by amniotic sac seized hold of the bottom and then pushed in opposite directions, opening Leonard's mouth almost to a breaking point. Some of Leonard's teeth, being as rotted and decayed as they were, broke off and were knocked to the back of his throat. Unable to close his mouth to spit them out, Leonard swallowed hard, tasting blood and feeling his teeth sliding down the back of his throat. Leonard couldn't scream and didn't know what the fuck was happening but managed to get to his feet. He tried to grab hold of the mass, which was steadily trying to claw its way into his mouth, but it was useless. Whatever it was, it was far too slick and slimy, and he could not get a firm grasp of it. As more of the mass was shoved further into his mouth, breaking off yet more teeth, Leonard ran under one of the few remaining lights in the alley, which is where he finally saw what was happening to him. Leonard looked down, and staring back at him from a tiny malformed skull were two tiny eyes that blinked. Leonard almost passed out, but just as he was beginning to fall to the ground, what was left of the gelatinous mass pulled itself into Leonard's mouth and began to squirm and slither down his throat. The last thing hanging out of Leonard's mouth and trailing down his chest was what appeared to be a long, thick strand of sickly gray spaghetti. Leonard grabbed it and pulled as hard as he could. It was then that he realized it wasn't spaghetti he had taken hold of; it was an umbilical cord. It slipped out of his hand into his mouth and slithered down his throat.

Leonard was finally able to take in a lung full of air, as the fetus had previously blocked his airway, and while he still wanted to pass out because of the absolute terror of what he was going though, he couldn't because his body was involuntarily gagging and heaving, trying to rid itself of the meal that had been force-fed into his mouth, over his tongue, past his throat, beyond his pharynx, down his esophagus, and finally past his esophageal sphincter and into his once empty stomach. Leonard could feel the thing moving in his stomach, twisting and turning as if it was trying to find a comfortable position. Although he was in complete shock, Leonard could not help but remember a movie he saw long ago. Something about a man who was impregnated with a creature that eventually burst forth in a shower of blood from the man's stomach and wreaked havoc aboard a spacecraft. Leonard could not help but wonder if that was to be his fate as well.

The fetus, having manipulated itself into the comfy, familiar darkness it had grown accustomed to prior to being so rudely ripped from its host, could now relax and get back to just being a baby, but something didn't feel right. Whatever fluid it was now in was nothing like the amniotic fluid it was familiar with. This fluid was beginning to burn and sting. This host was definitely not like the last one, and there was still an undeniable need to find its original host. "This can't be right," the fetus thought to itself. "This is not my host." With that, the fetus knew it had to leave. It knew that its original host was still out there somewhere and that it had to find her.

Leonard was frozen with fear, horrified at the thought of what was now settled in his overstuffed belly. He felt as if he had swallowed a whole chicken that was now sitting in his gut waiting to be digested. "I need to get to a hospital before whatever it was that just rammed its way down my throat does decide to exit by route of my belly button," Leonard thought to himself. Just as he was about to make his way to the closest emergency room, he felt movement in the pit of his stomach. The fetus was on the move again. It felt as if it were traveling up and then suddenly changed directions.

The fetus reached up and clawed the top of Leonard's stomach and was just about to exit via the same route it had entered, but while probing in the darkness of Leonard's innards, it found another hole down below. "Why go up when down was so much easier," thought the blob of baby parts, so it changed directions. Leonard felt the shift, then clutched his lower abdomen, and fell to the ground in agony. The fetus let go to the upper part of the stomach and proceeded to push and claw its way from the stomach, past the pyloric sphincter and into the duodenum, pushing digestive juice, chyme, and undigested food ahead of it and pulling placenta, amniotic sac and the rest of its baby body parts behind it. Leonard ripped at his torn and tattered shirt, exposing his sweaty, dirty stomach. He felt as if he was having the worst shit cramps ever. He pushed and prodded at his abdomen, trying to stop the thing, but it was useless. Leonard could only watch as he felt, and saw the mass moving from one side of his body to the other, as if it were on some twisting and turning roller coaster. The only difference was this roller coaster's track was about 25 feet long and neatly tucked inside Leonard's body. At one point, Leonard could have sworn that he saw the impression of a little misshapen face and skull pushing against his skin from the inside of his body.

The thing moved past his jejunum and then his ileum and finally entered his large intestine. Now, in addition to the other slop from Leonard's stomach and small intestine, the fetus found itself surrounded by all the fecal matter that was piled and compacted in Leonard's colon. It plowed forward pushing the feces ahead of it, giving Leonard an involuntary, from the inside out, reverse colonoscopy. The pain at this point was just about to send Leonard plunging into forever darkness, but before the darkness could consume him, the fetus hurtled up Leonard's ascending colon, shot across his transverse colon, plummeted down his descending colon, slithered the short distance across the sigmoid colon, and plopped down into his rectum, at which time Leonard's body cramped as if squeezed by a vise grip, then convulsed, and everything that was plowing through Leonard's body burst from his rectum with enough force to rip a hole in his threadbare pants. Leonard's baggy pants filled with fecal matter, the contents of his stomach, the blob of baby parts, and the last thing Leonard saw before death came for him were two little arms reaching out from the leg of his pants. A little deformed face looked back at him as it dragged itself out of his trousers and across his sneakers, leaving a trail of slime in its wake as it slithered into the night.

3

Ashley sat alone in her living room, eyes bloodshot from crying. Her best friend, Claire, stayed with her, trying to comfort her for a few hours after leaving the abortion clinic, but it was useless. Around midnight, Ashley finally told Claire that she wanted to be alone. "Call me if you need anything. I'll leave my phone on, just in case," said Claire; she then hugged Ashley and left. "What have I done?" thought Ashley to herself, as she lay down on the couch. Although she had contemplated for weeks about going through with the abortion, she couldn't help but feel that she somehow had made the wrong decision. Stranger still was the sensation that her now dead and decaying baby was somehow still with her. "Maybe this is normal," she thought to herself. "Maybe this feeling that my baby is still alive will pass in time." The tears started to fall again, and Ashley cried herself to sleep. That night, Ashley dreamt that she was still pregnant, her uterus still full and her belly still bulging. In the dream, she had awakened to use the bathroom in the

18

middle of the night; "like clockwork," Ashley thought to herself, 3:00 a.m., and here come the waterworks. She made her way to the bathroom, sat down, and started to do her business. As Ashley released the stream of pent-up urine from her bladder, she could see her stomach begin to deflate, like air being released from a balloon. At the same time, there was a plop into the water in the commode. Ashley panicked, stood up, and, thinking the worst, looked down into the bowl. It was empty. "My baby, where is my baby?" Ashley screamed, clutching at her now flat abdomen. Running to the bedroom, Ashley snatched her cell phone on the nightstand next to her bed. She trembled as she tried to dial 911; not knowing what else to do. She paused just as her finger was about to press the last digit on her touch pad and listened. She could have sworn that she heard crying. "Oh my God!" thought Ashley as she ran back into the bathroom, thinking that maybe her baby had somehow resurfaced in the toilet bowl. She fell to the floor, ready to scoop her baby out of the chilly, yellow tinted water, but there was nothing there.

Ashley, still kneeling on the bathroom floor sobbing, thought to herself, "What's happening? I must be losing my mind." Just as she was about to push herself from the floor, the crying started again. She paused, listening as hard as she could and trying to sense the direction from which the crying was coming. Standing now, she quietly walked into the hallway, which was dimly lit from the moonlight shining in from the bathroom window. Though her heart was pounding, Ashley listened intently, looking up and down the hall. "It's coming from the kitchen," Ashley thought to herself. She turned to her left and apprehensively walked toward the kitchen. The room was dimly lit from a small night light that was plugged into one of the sockets. Ashley stood in the doorway, looking around the room, her eyes finally stopping at the garbage pail. The crying was coming from the trash bin; but how? Ashley walked toward the garbage, which stank of the tuna she had yesterday for dinner. The crying intensified in volume. She hesitantly placed her foot on the plate to raise the lid of the bin and pushed down. The lid popped up, and staring back at Ashley from within was Ashley's broken and mangled baby. Parts of it was scattered around the pail like the pieces of a jigsaw puzzle. One arm climbing the side of the pail, the other one lying limply in an open can of peas. One bent and broken leg was barely visible in the corner of the pail, and the other was draped over a discarded bottle of water. The ripped torso and crushed head were smack dab in the middle of the pail. The head swiveled, looking up at Ashley. Its mouth opened and let out the most mournful, soul-wrenching sound she had ever heard in her entire life. Ashley jolted awake, drenched in sweat, screaming at the top of her lungs.

# 4

For the rest of the night, the fetus crawled uneventfully through the city, drawn ever onward by some undeniable force, slithering from shadow to shadow and keeping itself hidden from view whenever possible. After sunrise, it moved into the sewers to avoid the unrelenting blistering sun, which it noticed began to dry the moisture from its blob-like body. After a few hours of moving through the grimy and dirty underbelly of the city, the fetus sensed something moving up ahead. The fetus moved steadily forward, curious as to what it was. "Maybe it's my host," thought the tiny fetus. After rounding a bend in the sewer pipe, the fetus came face to face with a round, fuzzy creature with a bushy tail and a black mask of fur covering its eye area. The raccoon, seeing what looked like an easy meal coming around the corner, stopped. It hesitantly moved toward the fetus and sniffed at it. The fetus, knowing that this was definitely not an appropriate host, froze, curious about the creature it had come in contact with. After a few moments, the raccoon, feeling confident that the blob posed no immediate threat, chittered, calling over its two kits, which were not far away exploring. The kits, being naturally curious and extremely hungry, came over to examine the fleshy glob.

Tentatively, all three animals began to nibble at the pile, trying to pull off tiny pieces to guzzle down. One of the kits spied and sniffed at a fleshy, pink piece of meat and then took hold of it in its tiny mouth, which was filled with small, needle-sharp teeth. When the kit bit down on the fetus's arm, the fetus felt a stinging pain shoot through its entire body, which was still connected through a stretch of tangled and jumbled up nerves. The tiny arm, which was threaded with sinew, sprang out with remarkable speed, wrapped and twisted around the kit's body, and began to squeeze like a boa constrictor. The umbilical cord wasted no time in snagging the other kit, which managed only the smallest squeak before it, too, was restrained. All of this happened in a matter of seconds. The mother of the two baby raccoons jumped back, ready to attack and fight whatever this was to the death to defend her babies, but it was to no avail. With surprising speed, the fetus used the amniotic sac, which expanded like a parachute catching air. The sac stretched unnaturally wide over the top of the adult raccoon and then slid swiftly under its feet, engulfing the animal, which struggled in vain to detangle itself from the bubble of human flesh.

The sac began to draw back in on itself. At the same time, the arm and umbilical cord began to withdraw back into the mass, dragging all three besieged animals into the center of the bubble. Soon all three screeching and panicking animals found themselves trapped in the confines of a bubble-like amniotic sac the size of a large beach ball. All three scratched, clawed, and bit at the walls of the bubble in search of a way out. It was futile. Suddenly and without warning, the bubble began to contract, which caused an even greater panic for the raccoons. From the size of a beach ball, it continued to shrink down to the size of a basketball, allowing less and less room for the three captives. The bloody and veiny ball continued to shrivel, shrinking from the size of a basketball to the size of a soccer ball. At this point, movement for the family was nearly impossible. The ball grew smaller still, down to the size of a volleyball. At this point, there was no more struggling or fighting coming from the bubble. When the sac contracted yet again down to the size of a cabbage ball, there was one last high-pitched scream of pain from all three mammals and a sickening crunch of bones being shattered. The fetus, sensing that the threat had been eradicated, released its hold on the captives and slinked off into the sewer, leaving behind a twisted and mangled ball of fur, broken bones, and blood.

## 5

"I feel like shit," Dmitry told his best friend, Bryan. "I panicked, hell I hadn't heard from her in weeks; then she calls and tells me that she's pregnant." Dmitry looked down at the ground, embarrassed and unable to look his friend in the eye. "You should call her," said Bryan. "Call and say what, that I'm sorry for being a dick?" Brian looked at Dmitry and said, "Well, that's a start." The two friends had decided to go for a bike ride and were now sitting on a bench in the park where they often went riding. Dmitry looked out over the lake they were now sitting in front of. There were still quite a few people out canoeing, but they would all soon be heading in as the sun was just beginning to set. "I know, and that's exactly what I plan on doing." "The last thing I expected was a call telling me that I'm about to be a father," said Dmitry. Bryan, being the overtly blunt friend, said, "Maybe you should have thought about that before you decided to raw dog her." Dmitry looked at Bryan with some irritation and said, "Dude, you know, sometimes you can be a bit of a dick." Bryan laughed. "Come on, let's get out of here and head home."

Dmitry and Bryan parted ways, each heading toward his home. When Dmitry reached his place, he locked up his bike and walked up the two flights of stairs to his tiny apartment. "It's now or never," thought Dmitry. He sat on the couch, pulled out his cell phone, and dialed Ashley's number. The phone rang a couple of times before Ashley picked up. "Hello," Ashley said. "Hi, Ashley; it's Dmitry." Sile nce. At first, Dmitry thought that Ashley had hung up. "What do you want, Dmitry?" Ashley finally spoke, barely concealing the annoyance and anger she was feeling. "Look, I know how you must be feeling toward me and what you must be thinking about me, considering our last conversation, but I think we really need to get together and figure this out," said Dmitry. After more awkward and uncomfortable silence, Ashley finally said, "Yeah, I guess there is a lot we need to discuss." "Why don't you come by tomorrow morning, we can grab some breakfast and talk for a bit," said Ashley. Dmitry agreed and promised that he would call before heading over to her apartment. Then he hung up the phone.

# 6

After coming in contact with the raccoon, the fetus spent most of the daylight hours traveling underground, pulled ever onward toward its host. It was traveling through a large section in the underground sewer system and could sense night slowly approaching. Deciding to leave the twisting and turning labyrinth beneath the city to pursue a quicker and more direct route to its host, the fetus exited the sewer through a storm drain. Crawling vertically up the wall, sticking to it as easily as a spider to its web, the fetus climbed. Moving in rhythmic waves and contractions, it then squeezed through the grating in the drain. It emerged near a bus stop in a relatively quiet area of town. There were few passersby, and traffic on the road was sparse. It started to slink off in the direction of its unsuspecting host but was sidetracked by the scent of something interesting. Deciding to investigate, it slid off in the direction of the slightly familiar smell. It noticed a person similar to its host, but definitely not her, sitting on a bench under an awning on the corner. Next to the lady was a basket on wheels. The smell was coming from the basket. The person on the bench was utterly distracted by something in her hands, scarcely paying attention to her surroundings or to the basket she was sitting next to. The fetus reached the basket with ease, completely unnoticed. Its tiny skull tilted upward, and its undeveloped but sensitive ears picked up the tiniest of cooing noises coming from within the basket.

Latching onto the wheel of the stroller and wrapping itself around the leg like a creeper vine coiling around a dead tree trunk, the fetus slid higher and higher. Anxious to know what the noises coming from within basket were, the fetus stretched its placenta upward, pushing its malformed torso and head above the brink of the basket. Peering over the side, the fetus looked upon a form not unlike its own, the only difference being that the thing in the basket was whole and healthy. The infant in the basket stared back at the fetus, which now clinging to the side of the stroller, and gurgled. The fetus pulled the rest of its mass into the basket and moved back into the shadows, adhering to the underside of the stroller's canopy. The baby followed the fetus with its eyes, attempting to reach out to grab the thing that now shared its carriage space. Once the fetus was hidden away unseen above the baby's head, it began to examine the baby, reaching its little arms down like two slimy little snakes, caressing the infant's head and tiny appendages, which were soft and delicate, probably very easily broken. It extended its torso and head forward, sniffing the baby, which smelled of baby powder and scented wipes. Its mouth opened, and a miniature tongue slid out prodding the baby's face and briefly passing over the child's lips, where it faintly tasted the lingering flavor of breast milk.

Rage and bitterness replaced curiosity and wonder in an instant. "This should be me," thought the fetus. "This should be my life. Instead, my host, for whatever reason, decided not to give me a chance, decided not to give us a chance. Who knows, we could have had an amazing life together, but instead my host tried to destroy me." By this time, its frustration was at a boiling point. Its arms, still attached to the blob by tendons, placenta, and amniotic sac, stretched out, one arm wrapping itself under and then around the baby's neck and the other snaking around the baby's arm. It began to squeeze, gently. Its fight was not with this kindred spirit. The fetus dripped down from the canopy, nuzzled its deformed head next to the baby's head, both making contented, cooing sounds to one another. It unhappily released its hold on the infant and quietly made its way undetected out of the stroller and back onto the streets, leaving the side of the stroller facing away from the lady, and the baby inside covered in mucus and bloody residue. Its host wasn't far away, and the pull was growing stronger, the closer the two came to one another. The baby inside the stroller, now no longer distracted by his new friend and now uncomfortably wet, began to cry. "Hush, hush, Mommy is here," the lady said, and reached towards the stroller to comfort her child, never once looking away from the phone in her other hand. As her free hand fell upon the slimy canopy of the stroller she jerked it away in disgust. The lady finally tore her gaze from her cell phone and looked into the basket and gasped in horror at the red stains covering her baby's blanket and clothing. The lady stood up and took hold of her baby, looking him over with fear and confusion in her eyes and searching for the source of the bleeding but finding nothing. The baby was looking down at the ground, still crying hysterically and reaching out his tiny hands, curling and uncurling his little finger. The lady followed her baby's eyes and hands, looking for whatever it was that had the toddler so distracted. It was then that her eyes fell upon the fetus as it squirmed behind a row of bushes that were adjacent to the bus stop. The woman clutched her child to her breast and shrieked at the top of her lungs as she saw a little foot disappear into the shrubbery. She ran from the bus stop, finally forgetting the cell phone, which now lay broken and discarded on the ground next to the stroller.

## 7

Katrina, knowing it was going to be a long day, decided to dress comfortably. She threw on her favorite sundress, forgoing any kind of panties as the day promised to be a hot one. She met Joshua and Rebecca for brunch, and they all got started drinking early, each having a few rounds of mimosas. After brunch, they had planned to get out of the city for a bit, so everyone loaded into Joshua's truck and drove out to the lake to go fishing. At about 6 p.m., after sitting on the banks for a few hours, laughing and telling embarrassing stories and having finished off a bottle of fireball between the three of them, the trio decided to head back to the city. Joshua, being the most responsible of the three and knowing he had to drive home, took it easy on the shots and let the girls have all the fun. The group had tickets to an outdoor music festival which they had purchased weeks ago. They drank and danced to techno music well into the night; by 10 P.M., they were all wasted. As usual, Rebecca and Josh, who swore up and down that they were not into one another, started making out. Katrina, having been through this scenario far too many times before and not wanting to be the third wheel, said to herself, "I'm outta' here," and decided that she would stumble home to her apartment. Katrina decided against telling Josh and Rebecca that she was leaving. She knew that if she did they would have to cut their night short to walk her home. They both looked as if they were having a blast, so she didn't want to ruin it for them. "I'll just call Rebecca when I'm home," Katrina thought to herself. "She'll be pissed and probably curse me out for walking home alone in my current inebriated state, but it'll be too late for her to do anything about it." With Joshua and Rebecca preoccupied, tongue wrestling one another, Katrina saw her chance for escape and slipped through the crowd toward her apartment.

The walk to her apartment was about eight blocks, which was going to take forever, or she could just cut through the park, which would save her about twenty minutes. Katrina stood at the entrance of the park weighing her options. She knew that the park was pretty well lit, and, more often than not, there would be the occasional couple strolling through, holding hands and looking for a dark, secluded niche in which to make out. She had walked through the park many times before, without incident, and knew the area pretty well, so with that in mind and fueled by liquid courage, she made up her mind and decided to chance the shortcut. Katrina stumbled onto the tree-lined pathway and began to make her way deeper into the park. After a few minutes of walking, the shadows of the trees began to blend into the blackness of the night, muffling the sounds of the busy city. As the sounds of the city disappeared and were replaced by the stillness of the park, Katrina froze in place. "What the hell was that?" she said to herself. She could hear the snapping of branches and the crunch of dead leaves, as if something small was moving through the underbrush just beyond the pathway tree line. In addition to the scraping sound, Katrina thought she heard crying. She listened harder, and now she could definitely make out a gentle cooing and gurgling, the undeniable sounds of a baby coming from somewhere close by, which freaked her out and partially sobered her up. She assumed in horror that someone must have abandoned some poor, innocent baby here in the park, and without a second thought Katrina stepped off the pathway and began walking in the direction of the sound.

# 8

The fetus, after leaving the carriage and reluctantly parting from its newfound friend, had made its way undisturbed through the streets and now found itself in another section of the city, which was dark, seemingly deserted, and overgrown with trees and other foliage. It was much easier to travel unnoticed here, moving from tree to tree but ever onward in the direction of its host. It could tell it was drawing nearer its host as the pull was becoming stronger with each undulation of its gelatinous form. As the fetus was dragging its body over, through, and around the tree roots it was now traversing, it froze and listened. Something was moving through the trees not far off. Deciding it was better to avoid any unnecessary interaction and anxious to finally face its host, the fetus began to slowly slither away from whatever it was that was approaching.

It was disturbingly dark, and Katrina had to stop a few times to reorient herself and determine from which direction the baby noises were coming from. As impossible as it seemed, the noise seemed to be moving. After a few minutes of searching, the sounds Katrina was tracking stopped. Just ahead, about 15 feet in front of her, Katrina could barely discern something scoot behind the trunk of a large oak tree, leaving a trail of wetness in its wake. A disturbing thought entered Katrina's mind: "What if a dog or some other animal had gotten hold of the baby and was trying to drag it off to eat it?" Katrina shivered and tried to shake off the terribly disturbing image of a pack of wild dogs feasting on baby body parts that now flashed through her mind. As she cautiously approached the tree, fearful of some vicious animal attacking her for trying to steal its dinner, Katrina could see a tiny little leg hiked up on a tree root. She placed a hand on the tree and warily leaned her body against it, looking down and preparing herself for the worse.

Nothing could have readied Katrina for the atrocity she saw. It was indeed a baby, but the poor thing was ripped and torn to shreds. The world spun and Katrina felt her eyes fill with tears; she was just about to bend down to get a closer look at the thing on the ground at her feet when it moved. Surely the movement was a trick of the moonlight shining through the thick canopy of tree tops and falling on the grotesque mess before her. Before she could do anything further, the head of the baby twisted on its neck, the mouth opened, and the thing started to cry. Katrina shrieked and fell backwards, her foot snagging on a raised tree root, and hit her head on the tree directly behind her. This time the world went black as Katrina was knocked unconscious from the impact. When she landed, her legs were spread apart, and her sundress flew up, revealing the dark wrinkle of her vagina.

The fetus inch-wormed itself from behind the oak, clambering over one of Katrina's legs, leaving a wet, bloody trail across her upper thigh. It was about to continue over her other leg in the direction of its host but stopped when it drew nearer Katrina's slightly parted vagina. A sense of familiarity and longing swept over the fetus, and though the call was still pulling it onward, it thought to itself that maybe its search could be over. Maybe it could abandon its pursuit for the host that had discarded it like last night's leftovers and instead merge with and continue its development with someone who actually wanted it. Sure the first host it tried to enter was definitely not a good match, but something about this host felt "right." The fetus extended one arm like an octopus toward Katrina's opening and parted the left side of her labia; the other hand reached out and parted the right side. Katrina stirred but did not awaken from her slumber. The fetus pushed its hands in opposite direction, which revealed that Katrina's vaginal canal was just wide enough for it to squeeze itself into. It could see nothing beyond the blackness of her opening, but it knew instinctively that this was the right way to go. First its head, shoulder and torso were forced into Katrina's opening, and then the rest of the placenta and amniotic sac, along with both legs, were dragged in behind it. The arms and hands were the last to enter as they stayed behind to hold her labia open. Once inside Katrina's vaginal

41

canal, the fetus continued upward, squeezing its body parts and placenta past her cervix and finally into the uterus.

"Ahhhh . . . , now this feels much more comfortable than that first host I entered," thought the fetus as it circled around starting to get comfortable in Katrina's uterus and bulging out of her lower pelvic area just a bit. The pressure of the newly implanted mass and the cold air flowing across Katrina's wet and bloodied thigh began to stir her from her unwanted sleep. She slowly opened her eyes, looking up at the tree tops above her. Then images of the broken and bloody baby came flooding back to her. Katrina bolted upright, looking around in a panic for any signs of the infant. Immediately, her hands went between her legs where she felt the moisture coating her legs and vagina. Upon drawing her hand back, she could see in the moonlight that it was covered in blood. Katrina had no idea what was happening and was pushing herself up from off the ground when a stabbing pain ripped through her pelvic area. She fell back to the ground and grabbed at her lower abdomen, which is when she noticed the strange lump that had not been there before she was knocked unconscious. She pushed at the knot, and at the same time the lump seemed to push back at her hand, and more stabbing pain almost made her black out again. Confused and frightened, she said aloud: "What the fuck is happening to me?" She lifted her sundress enough, so that she could see a hand-sized lump on her lower abdomen. She figured that she must have hit her abdomen on a root or branch when she was knocked out. Though it was dark, Katrina could see the lump moving back and forth under her skin, which was the cause of the unbelievable pain she was again experiencing.

Although the space now occupied by the fetus was indeed comfortable and semi-familiar, it had assumed the pull it was feeling would cease with the occupation of a new host, but it did not. The need to pursue its original host was still there and stronger than ever. It did not fade as the fetus had anticipated it would. Considering that denying the

43

call was not an option, the fetus knew it had to leave the relative safety and warmth of Katrina's vagina. With that in mind, it started the short journey to exit the same way it came in. Katrina looked in revulsion at the lump that had mysteriously appeared in her pelvic area, which was now somehow moving. She was frozen in fear and could only stare in horror at the floating mass. Though the wriggling mass felt uncomfortable, the unbearable pain she previously felt did not accompany its movement this time. Katrina parted her legs and looked down at her vagina with dread, knowing the moving thing could only exit her body one possible way.

The fetus reversed its previous course, moving from Katrina's uterus, past her cervix into her vaginal canal, and finally used its little hands to once again part her labia. At the emergence of the tiny, deformed skull from Katrina's vagina, her voice was loosened. Katrina screamed at the top of her lungs as the fetus dragged itself from her body. Katrina kicked her legs and scraped her buttocks and hands bloody as she crawfished backwards over tree roots, trying to put as much distance as she could between herself and the monstrosity that she had unwillingly birthed. Katrina sat on the cold, hard ground hugging her knees to her chest, staring in utter disbelief and disgust at the thought of what was happening to her. The fetus looked back at her, let out a deplorable wail of sadness, and then glided off in pursuit of what it now knew to be its original and only acceptable host. Although Katrina was appalled at what had just happened, in the short period of time the fetus had occupied her body, she felt a connection with the thing. She knew what happened to it and could not help but feel sorrow and pity for the thing that only desired to be loved and wanted. Katrina, vowing to never speak a word of what happened to anyone, stood up, wiped away the tears that were unknowingly streaming down her cheeks, dusted her clothes off as best as she could, and continued her journey home.

## 9

It was a little past midnight, and Ashley had just made it home after an emotionally draining day. She had met with Claire after work to have a few drinks. She had not been sleeping well since the night of the abortion and figured that the drinks she had earlier in evening would help her to finally get a good night's rest. After coming home and undressing, Ashley sat on the sofa and randomly flipped through the channels, stopping on one that was playing reruns of *Charmed*, which was one of her all-time favorite TV shows. She had plans to meet up with Dmitry at 7 A.M. so that she could tell him what she had done and be done with him once and for all. Finding herself nodding off on the couch, Ashley decided to take a shower and call it a night. Never liking the house to be silent, Ashley left the TV on and headed to the bathroom to take a nice long shower.

"I'm close," thought the fetus to itself, finally making it out of the park and back onto the city streets. It slinked along the curbsides avoiding any further contact with anyone until it found itself in a residential area. The neighborhood was quiet, with a mix of cozy single-family homes and a small apartment complex occupying the end of the street. Ashley lived in the complex, occupying an end unit on the second floor. Her bedroom window overlooked a small bayou, and she always slept with the window open so that she could listen to the nighttime sounds coming off the bayou. The fetus crept through the neighborhood, finally making its way to the apartment complex, and made a beeline toward the building where Ashley lived. It arrived at the bottom of the stairway leading up to her unit and, like a slinky in reverse, slinked up to the top of the stairs. It crawled to her front door and searched for a way in, probing at the edges of the doorway in vain. It abandoned its inspection of the door and moved down the walkway. When it reached the edge, it slipped under the railing and rounded the edge of the building, sticking to the side of the building like a slug. There was a window a little higher up. The fetus reached the window and peeked in. The room was sparsely furnished with random furniture and a television set showing a group of ladies using powers to fend off a large red and black demon that was throwing energy balls at them. The fetus soon discovered that this entry point was sealed just as tightly as the door was. Looking around, the fetus spied another window further down the building. It made its way to the next window and was in luck. This window was open, with nothing but a flimsy screen blocking entry to the apartment. The fetus easily ripped a hole in the netting and crawled through the window into Ashley's bedroom.

Ashley turned on her Kate Bush Pandora station, connected it to her wireless Bluetooth radio, and stepped into the shower. She was standing under the stream of the shower singing along to "Wuthering Heights"; listening to Kate always made Ashley feel better. Not many millennials could appreciate the musical surrealism of the legendary Kate. The room had become steamy, and Ashley was so caught up in her rendition of the song that she did not notice the blob that had quietly found its way into the bathroom with her. Through the clear shower curtain, the fetus finally laid eyes on its host and was filed with rage. All the hatred and betrayal it felt for its host came flooding back to it. It was so close and would finally have revenge on the host who had sought to destroy it. The fetus crawled to the back of the bathtub and effortlessly glided up the wall and onto the ceiling.

Ashley, face upturned to the warm stream of water dancing from the shower head, eyes shut tight in an attempt to keep out the shampoo, did not see the thing that was quietly stalking her. The blob of fetus body parts was directly above Ashley in the shower and began to lower its two arms down toward her with every intention of wrapping them around Ashley's neck and choking the life out of her. Just before the snake-like appendages reached the top of Ashley's head, she finished rinsing the shampoo from her eyes and opened them. What she saw when she opened her eyes made her blood run cold. She opened her mouth to scream, which is when the thing that was hanging above her released its grip on the ceiling and fell directly onto her face. The fetus, upon landing on Ashley's face, wrapped its placenta and amniotic sac around her chin, mouth, and face and then whipped its umbilical cord around her neck and began to squeeze. Ashley slipped and fell, grabbing the shower curtain and pulling it off the rod as she tumbled out of the tub and landed in a heap on the bathroom floor. Ashley was in a blind panic and tried in vain to rip whatever it was that was attacking her away from her face. She stood up, clawing at her head, face, and neck; then she flew to the mirror, which was clouded over with steam from the shower. She could not see much, as part of the mass covered one of her eyes when it wrapped itself around her head. Whatever this was, its grip around her neck began to tighten, tiny pinpoints of light began to swim in front her eyes and Ashley knew that she did not have much time left before she blacked out. She ran from the bathroom to her bedroom and tripped on the rug as she entered, knocking over the lamp from her night stand. She crashed to the ground, still trying to pull the thing away from her mouth. She sat up, back against the bed, and realized that her vision from the one eye that was still uncovered began to narrow and grow dark; she was on the point of passing out and it wouldn't be long before she lost consciousness. Just then the thing loosened its grip on her neck, and one coil slipped away from her mouth. The fetus did not want its host to die without being aware of exactly why she had to die. It extended its torso and misshapen head forward so that Ashley could get a good look at it. When it came into her field of vision, she almost passed out from the sheer terror of what she saw. The fetus looked into Ashley's eye and croaked out one shocking word, "Mommy."

Ashley's heart broke like never before, and she knew instantaneously what the thing wrapped around her head trying to kill her was; it was her aborted baby. She continued to feel such a connection with her baby because it was, by some mysterious force, still alive. Tears streamed down

Ashley's face at the realization of why this was happening to her. Instinctively, she knew that the baby she had tried to destroy had come back for its revenge, although Ashley did not think she should die because of the decision she had made. She thought it to be the right decision at the time she made it. She nonetheless understood why her baby thought she should die. As she resigned herself to the death she would soon face, she looked at her baby, who was deformed and mutilated, seemingly beyond repair; with heartfelt sadness and remorse, she whispered: "I'm so sorry, my baby. I love you." With that she closed her eyes and waited for the crushing force around her neck to resume. A few seconds ticked by, then a few more, and suddenly Ashley felt her baby completely unwrap itself from around her face and neck, and with a plop it fell onto the ground next to her. She cautiously opened her eyes and looked down. The blob of baby parts was on the ground, reaching out to her and crying for her to pick it up. The image of this thing on the floor, rather than the stuff nightmares are born of, was for Ashley more adorable than anything she had ever seen before.

Ashley reached down, and the baby crawled into her open arms. She knew that her baby sensed the remorse she had felt for trying to have it aborted, and it had forgiven her. She cradled the mass to her, hardly aware of the sticky mess it left all over her face and body. Her baby stretched out its tiny arms and wrapped them around Ashley's neck as she held its torso and head against her breast. This time the baby squeezed Ashley's neck with love. The two stayed this way for a few minutes until the baby released its hold on Ashley, at which time she also released her grip. Ashley leaned down and kissed her baby softly on its tiny malformed head just before it slipped down past her breast, sliding down her abdomen and finally coming to a stop on the floor between her legs. Ashley wasn't quite sure what was happening as the baby spread its arms, pushed her legs apart, and then turned its attention to her vagina.

The baby knowingly spread her labia, and, though Ashley was confused, she now knew that her baby no longer meant her any harm. Feeling that something important was about to happen, she sat there with her legs parted and waited. Once her labia were parted and the vaginal canal was visible, the baby pushed its way in, which made Ashley recoil. First, the head and torso went in, followed by the legs, the placenta, amniotic sac, umbilical cord, and finally its little arms. Once the baby had entered and made its way up her vaginal canal, past her cervix and into her uterus, something started to happen, and though Ashley could not see it, she could definitely feel it. When the baby made its way into the uterus, the torn and tattered placenta began to heal and reattach to the uterine wall. The amniotic sac re-formed into a perfect little bubble, then refilled with fluid, and the broken and ripped fetus body parts also began to mend within the sac. Like air being blown into a deflated balloon, all the indentations in the baby's skull popped out, and soon the tiny skull was smooth and round again.

The crooked and broken arms and legs reattached and fused back onto its torso, broken bones mending, becoming whole and healthy again. Lastly, the dangling umbilical cord slithered snake-like from the baby's abdomen and attached itself to the placenta, and with that, Ashley had the world first unbortion. During the process, Ashley could sense something happening within her body and stared in wonder as her belly expanded. There was no pain accompanying the re-formation, and when it was complete, she knew without a doubt that she was once again 24 weeks pregnant with a strong and healthy baby growing inside her.

It was just after 2 A.M., still hours before Dmitry would be arriving. Ashley knew that she would not be getting any sleep tonight after what had just happened to her. She pushed up from the floor and cleaned up, picking up the broken lamp she had knocked over and fixing up the bathroom. She decided to finish her shower, which interrupted, and then she sat on the sofa, rubbing her swollen belly, lost in thought. Hours passed by like minutes, and there was a knock at the door. Ashley looked, and it was just after 7:30 in the morning. She stood up, walked to the door, dressed in pajama bottoms and a top that showed the slight bulge of her belly. She opened the door and greeted Dmitry with a smile; he stood there looking sheepish. "Come in," Ashley said. Dmitry entered, and they sat on the couch. After a few minutes of awkward silence, Dmitry said, "We need to talk." He apologized for the way he had handled things and asked for forgiveness for being such an ass. He continued: "I know that we don't really know one another, but I am not going to leave you alone in this. Regardless of whether you want to pursue a relationship with me or not, I am not going to let you face this alone." Ashley smiled and said "Thank you, I'm sure we can figure this out together." Dmitry sighed and relaxed a bit, then said, "Thank God, I was worried you had done something crazy, like have an abortion or something." Ashley smiled, placed a hand on her belly, and said, "Now why would I do something as foolish as that?"